TIMMY FISHES

SHARK ISLAND

To my neighbors,
Enjoy the story!

Written by
T.A. LOWELL

Illustration by
YAROSLAV CHYZHEVSKYI

Special thanks to Yaroslav and Bryony for bringing this story to life on the page and making it beautiful. To my children, Gus, Yara, Sophie, Sam, Emma and Isabella for smiling through every telling. And to all of the students and campers who showed enthusiasm for the stories and inspired me to write them down.

First published in 2021

Written by T.A. Lowell
Illustrated by Yaroslav Chyzhevskyi
Page design by Bryony van der Merwe

ISBN: 978-2-7374239-1-1 (hardcover edition)
ISBN: 978-1-7374239-0-4 (paperback edition)
ISBN: 978-1-7374239-2-8 (electronic edition)

Published by:

Active Art & Science

http://www.activeartandscience.com
Author page: http://www.talowell.com

To Mary,
Without your love and support
this story would not have
been written!

IT WAS STILL DARK

as I pedaled from my house to
the Berkeley Marina.

I had no idea this was the day I would
ALMOST BE EATEN ALIVE.

MY NAME IS TIMMY.

I'm the deckhand on a deep-sea fishing boat.
My job is to prepare the bait, tie hooks, untangle
lines, handle fish and keep the boat in ship shape.
I have worked summers and weekends at sea
since I was young.

Our boat is called JAWS, she is painted with
fierce eyes, ferocious teeth
and looks like
A GIANT SHARK
when she speeds through the water.

On this day, we were fishing at the Farallon Islands, about 30 miles off the coast of San Francisco. The islands are **craggy, windswept and a bit spooky.**

Native Ohlone people called them *the islands of the dead,* and mariners refer to them as *the devil's teeth.*

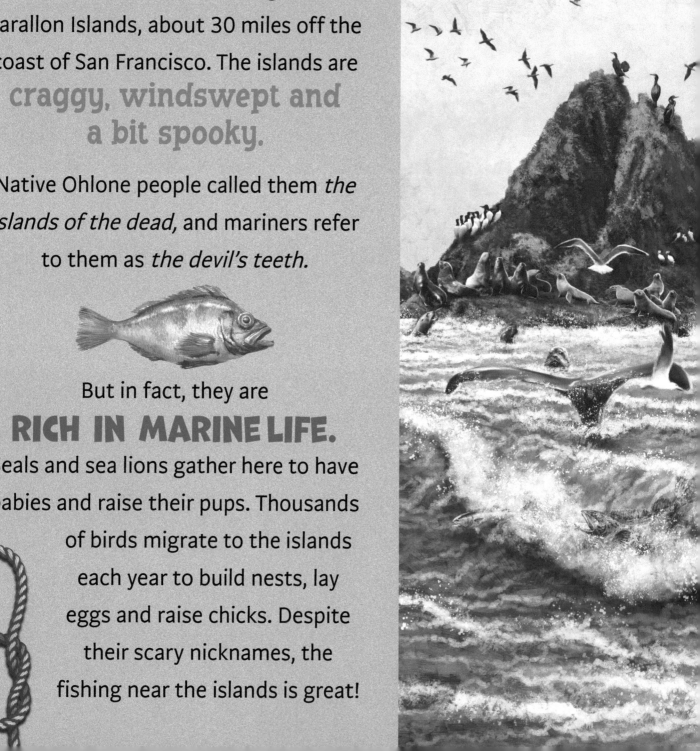

But in fact, they are

RICH IN MARINE LIFE.

Seals and sea lions gather here to have babies and raise their pups. Thousands of birds migrate to the islands each year to build nests, lay eggs and raise chicks. Despite their scary nicknames, the fishing near the islands is great!

We were catching big lingcod, one after another.

A lingcod is a dinosaur-like fish with a
**spiky head, big bulging eyes, flat nose
and a huge jaw full of sharp pointy teeth.**
Its head is like a boulder, its belly is fat, and its body is
rich in prized meat.

A very special lady, Mrs. Johnson, was fishing with us that Wednesday. She was almost 80 years old, **super strong and an expert fisherperson. She had a fishing rod as thick as a tree branch and a reel the size of my head.**

Mrs. Johnson would lay that rod on the rail of the boat and pull up

5, 6, 7

fish at a time. She always caught more than anyone else.

Suddenly I heard Mrs. Johnson shout,

"TIMMY, TIMMY, HELP!

Something's got my line, I can't hold on to it!"

Her line pulled tight under the boat and her big fishing rod was about to be pulled right out of her hands.

"I think it's caught on the bottom," I shouted. "Let me check."

I grabbed the rod and pulled back hard.

To my surprise, something on the other side of the fishing line **pulled back even harder!**

I had no idea what Mrs. Johnson had hooked.

"We'll have to break the line," I yelled.

"That's fine," she yelled back.

I pointed the rod straight down at the water and pulled with all my might, hoping the line would break.

While I was busy doing this, the line stopped pulling. It had not broken and there was still something crazy heavy on the other end, but now I could reel it in.

CRANKITY...

CRANKITY...

CRANKITY, I cranked...

...until, suddenly, a giant lingcod head appeared on the end of the line, like a stone with teeth.

Attached, but just barely, was...

A SKELETON!

Something had taken all the meat off the lingcod body but left the bones whole. It looked like a creature from a Halloween haunted house.

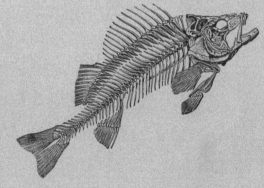

We were stunned, staring at that lingcod carcass, wondering what happened. Then...silently...rising from the depths of the ocean, came the **biggest great white shark I had ever seen.** My heart pounded wildly as the beast moved closer!

It was a massive creature, more than 20 feet long, with rows of teeth like daggers. I was an arms-length away from it.

If I had been in the water I could have been **chomped and eaten in two bites!**

Suddenly another huge great white shark rose up next to the first one. I realized they wanted their lingcod back. My hands were shaking as I threw the head and skeleton to them.

They stared at me one more time, took the gift and swam away. I wondered if this was why the Farallon Islands were called *islands of the dead?*

I never again came so close to great white sharks, although I saw plenty of them from a distance. Every Fall season a large group of sharks gather at the Farallon Islands to feast; it is often called a shark party by scientists. When I fish near the islands from September to December, I always make sure I bring something to share.

WHAT'S FOR DINNER?

Young sharks feast on fish and other small sea creatures. Grown-up sharks also add seals, sea lions and small whales to their diet. They do not hunt people! In the rare case of a person getting bitten, it is because the shark mistook them for a marine mammal. They might take one taste (yuck, ptooey!) and spit it out before they swim away. Great white sharks often sneak under their prey, then swim straight up at high-speed, causing them to burst out of the water.

MY, WHAT SHARP TEETH YOU HAVE!

Great white sharks have several rows of teeth. When a front tooth falls out or breaks, it is replaced by one of the back teeth. These sharks don't chew with their teeth; they use them to chop prey into pieces, which they swallow whole!

BASED ON A TRUE STORY

This book is based on a true story, I hope you enjoy reading it!

Timmy –
F/V Wild Wave

Timmy with salmon –
F/V New Capt. Pete

Big salmon – F/V New
Capt. Pete

Left: Timmy – F/V New Sea Wolf – sketch by Harry Lowell

Below: After the trip, F/V Jaws – Mrs. Johnson (far left), Timmy (lifting lingcod)

CPSIA information can be obtained
at www.ICGtesting.com
Printed in the USA
LVHW071242260621
691173LV00003B/43